W9-DAJ-672

SUPER RABBIT RACERS!

READ MORE
PRESS START!
BOOKS!

MORE COMING SOON!

PRESS START!

SUPER RABBIT RACERS!

THOMAS
FLINTHAM

BRANCHES

SCHOLASTIC INC.

FOR TOM R. AND EDDIE P.

Library of Congress Cataloging-in-Publication Data

Names: Flintham, Thomas, author, illustrator.
Title: Super Rabbit racers / by Thomas Flintham.
Description: First edition. | New York : Branches/Scholastic Inc., 2017. |
Series: Press start! ; 3 | Summary: Super Rabbit Boy is racing in the
Super Grand Prix car race—but among the other racers is King Viking and
his team of cheaters, and they will do anything to win.
Identifiers: LCCN 2016056221 | ISBN 9781338034790 (hardcover) |
ISBN 9781338034776 (pbk.)
Subjects: LCSH: Superheroes—Juvenile fiction. | Supervillains—Juvenile
fiction. | Video games—Juvenile fiction. | Animals—Juvenile fiction. |
Racing—Juvenile fiction. | CYAC: Superheroes—Fiction. |
Supervillains—Fiction. | Video games—Fiction. | Animals—Fiction. |
Automobile racing—Fiction.
Classification: LCC PZ7.1.F585 Sw 2017 | DDC [Fic]—dc23 LC record available at https://lccn.loc.gov/2016056221

10 9 8 7 6 5 4 3 2 1   17 18 19 20 21

Printed in China   38

First edition, November 2017
Edited by Celia Lee
Book design by Baily Crawford

TABLE OF
CONTENTS

Welcome to the Super Cup Grand Prix! In the Super Cup Grand Prix, racers compete in four races to win points.

The racer with the most points at the end wins the Super Cup! The cup is a special power up that gives the winner the power of super speed.

Who will win the Grand Prix and the Super Cup this time?

Let's meet the racers!

NAME:
SUPER RABBIT BOY

LIKES:
BEING A HERO

NAME:
SIMON THE
HEDGEHOG

LIKES:
BEING FAST

NAME:
KING VIKING

LIKES:
BEING MEAN

NAME:
PRINCESS PIRATE

LIKES:
CHEATING

NAME:
JODY RACER

LIKES:
WINNING

NAME:
FROG KNIGHT

LIKES:
BEING BRAVE

NAME:
ROBO BOBO

LIKES:
THROWING THINGS

NAME:
NUGGET

LIKES:
BEING A CHICKEN

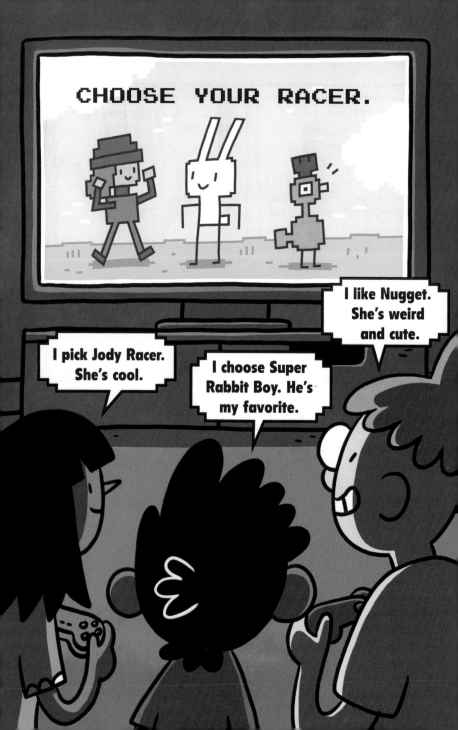

The first race is in Animal Town. Everyone gathers to cheer on the racers at the starting line. The countdown begins: 3 . . . 2 . . . 1 . . .

GO! Everyone speeds into action.

King Viking, Robo Bobo, and Princess
Pirate are at the back of the pack. It looks
like they have a plan. What are they doing?

Suddenly, Robo Bobo extends his Robo-arms. They're super long! He grabs Simon the Hedgehog and throws him off the course.

Then Princess Pirate bashes Frog Knight with her car's super secret boxing glove.

3 TRICKS AND TRAPS

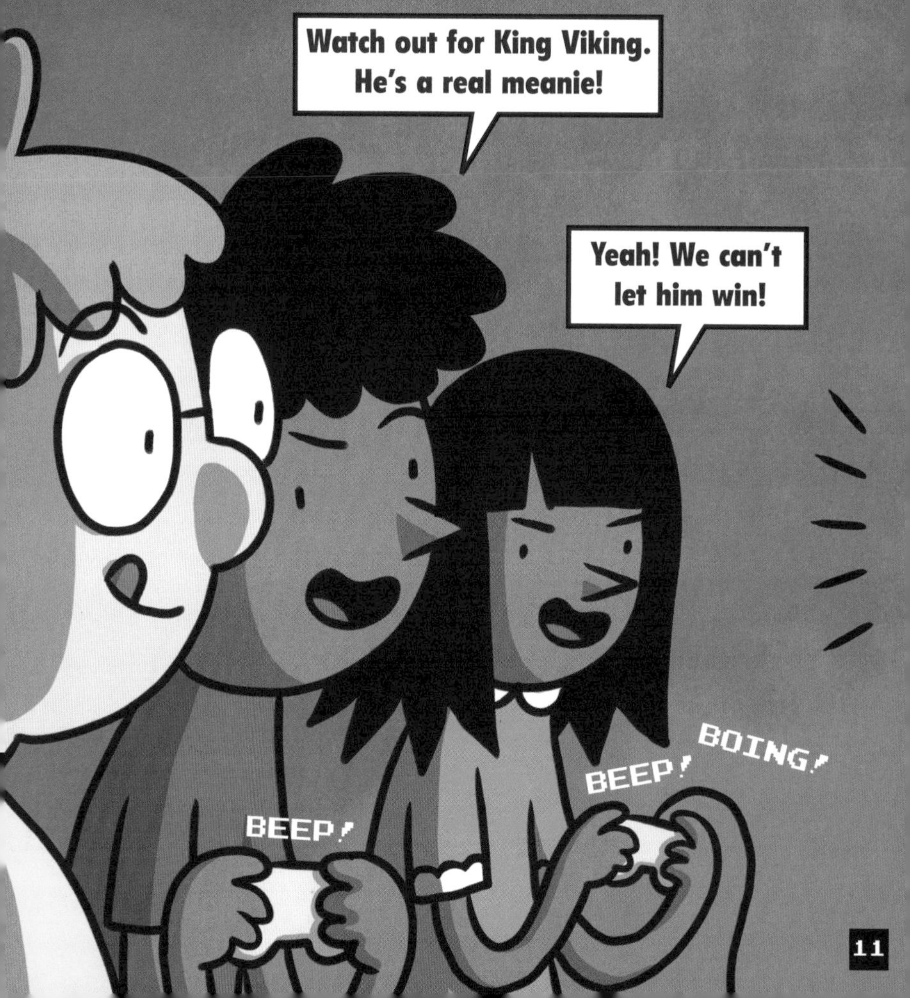

Robo Bobo reaches for Jody Racer. She dodges his long Robo-arms!

You'll have to try harder than that to catch me!

BOOP! BEEP! BOOP!

Meanwhile, Princess Pirate tries to stop Nugget with her super-secret boxing glove. Nugget weaves back and forth on the road. Princess Pirate can't catch her!

Hey! Drive straight so I can bop you!

Cluck! Cluck!

13

King Viking catches up with Super Rabbit Boy. He uses his car's special power. Giant fireballs come bursting out of his car!

Take that, Smelly Rabbit Boy!

The fireballs are blocking the road! How will Super Rabbit Boy get past them? Luckily, his car has a special power, too.

Super Rabbit Boy's car can jump! He jumps over the fireballs in one giant hop!

Team Viking has failed to stop the three racers. Soon the racers near the finish line.

Jody Racer is the first to cross the line. Super Rabbit Boy zooms across in second place. And Nugget weaves across in third place.

Princess Pirate and Robo Bobo stop their
cars so King Viking can pass them.

King Viking comes in fourth place. He is
not happy.

4 BIG BIG MOUNTAIN

Here are the racers' scores at the end of the first race:

-THE SCORES-

1 JODY RACER................. 9 POINTS
2 SUPER RABBIT BOY......... 6 POINTS
3 NUGGET..................... 3 POINTS
4 KING VIKING.............. 1 POINT
5 PRINCESS PIRATE........... 0 POINTS
6 ROBO BOBO................. 0 POINTS
7 FROG KNIGHT.............. 0 POINTS
8 SIMON THE HEDGEHOG...... 0 POINTS

The second race is on Big Big Mountain, home of the Big Big Giants. Who will be the first to reach the top of the mountain? 3 . . . 2 . . . 1 . . . GO!

Team Viking starts bashing and crashing into the other racers right away.

Soon they're in the front. They block the road so no one can get ahead.

Simon the Hedgehog makes a move! He tries to dash past them. He dodges Robo Bobo's grabbing Robo-arms.

But he runs straight into Princess Pirate's boxing glove.

Robo Bobo and Princess Pirate are so busy with Simon that the other racers slip past them. But King Viking is ready. He fires lots of fireballs toward the oncoming racers.

You can't pass me!

Nugget weaves between all the fireballs.
Go, Nugget!

But instead of passing King Viking,
Nugget weaves off the road! She falls into a
hole in the ground.

Poor Nugget.

Super Rabbit Boy, Jody Racer, and
Frog Knight have passed King Viking and
his fireballs. They're near the top of the
mountain. It's the final climb to the finish
line. The racers swoop around the last
corner.

There are Big Big Giants everywhere!

The giants' clomping feet stomp all around the racers. Frog Knight swerves away from one of the Big Big Giants. But he loses control of his car and drives off the side of the road!

Super Rabbit Boy, Jody Racer, and King Viking see the finish line.

Suddenly, a Big Big Giant steps in front of King Viking.

King Viking swerves out of the way . . .
right in front of Super Rabbit Boy!

Super Rabbit Boy hops over King Viking . . .

But he lands on Jody Racer! Oh no!

Jody Racer spins off the side of the road. But Super Rabbit Boy bounces over the finish line. He wins first place!

King Viking has crossed the finish line!

Suddenly, Nugget zooms out of a hole near the finish line. She crosses the line and speeds straight into King Viking!

Nugget is in third place.

Jody stomps up to Super Rabbit Boy. She is not happy!

6 SKYWAY HIGHWAY

Here are the scores at the end of the second race:

-THE SCORES-

```
1 SUPER RABBIT BOY......(+9)   15 POINTS
2 JODY RACER............(+0)    9 POINTS
3 KING VIKING...........(+6)    7 POINTS
4 NUGGET................(+3)    6 POINTS
5 SIMON THE HEDGEHOG...(+1)    1 POINTS
6 ROBO BOBO.............(+0)    0 POINTS
7 PRINCESS PIRATE.......(+0)    0 POINTS
8 FROG KNIGHT...........(+0)    0 POINTS
```

The third race is along the Skyway
Highway. It's a road in the clouds!
3 . . . 2 . . . 1 . . . GO!

Once again, Team Viking causes trouble
from the start. King Viking storms into first
place. Princess Pirate and Robo Bobo block
the other racers again.

Jody quickly speeds past the two trouble-makers. She's so fast! She quickly races toward King Viking.

BEEP! BEEP!

Yo ho! Jody may have passed us, but the rest of you won't be so lucky!

The rest of the racers are determined to get past. But when any of the racers try, Princess Pirate's boxing glove stops them.

And Robo Bobo is always ready with his long Robo-arms.

The racers are stuck!

Together, Robo Bobo and Princess Pirate keep the other racers back throughout the race.

Meanwhile, King Viking and Jody Racer
battle for first place.

The finish line is close. This race is almost
over! Who will win?

7 TWISTS AND TURNS

Super Rabbit Boy sees the finish line coming up.

> Oh, bloop! This is bad! I need to get past Team Viking and catch up!

Super Rabbit Boy springs into action! He drives up to the gap between Princess Pirate and Robo Bobo. The boxing glove and Robo-arms reach for him, but Super Rabbit Boy hops out of the way.

He made it! Super Rabbit Boy waves back before he zooms after King Viking and Jody Racer. Go, Super Rabbit Boy!

Super Rabbit Boy catches up to Jody Racer.

Just as he's right beside her, Jody pushes a button on her bike. It turns on her bike's secret turbo boosters!

BANG!!!

The turbo boosters blast Jody Racer toward the finish line. And Super Rabbit Boy gets blasted backward!

Jody zooms ahead at turbo speed. She almost passes King Viking, but he speeds across the finish line first!

46

Here are the scores after the third race.
King Viking is in the lead!

```
                    -THE SCORES-

1 KING VIKING..........(+9)   16 POINTS
2 JODY RACER...........(+6)   15 POINTS
3 SUPER RABBIT BOY.....(+0)   15 POINTS
4 NUGGET...............(+3)    9 POINTS
5 SIMON THE HEDGEHOG...(+1)    2 POINTS
6 ROBO BOBO............(+0)    0 POINTS
7 PRINCESS PIRATE......(+0)    0 POINTS
8 FROG KNIGHT..........(+0)    0 POINTS
```

SUPER CUP STADIUM

The fourth and final race is in Super Cup Stadium. The crowd cheers loudly, but the racers are nervous. King Viking cannot win! 3 . . . 2 . . . 1 . . . GO!

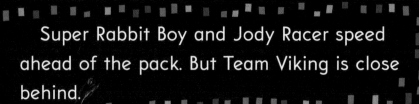
Super Rabbit Boy and Jody Racer speed ahead of the pack. But Team Viking is close behind.

I need to win this race! Then the power of super speed will be ALL MINE! You two must stop Super Rabbit Boy and Jody Racer!

Princess Pirate and Robo Bobo spring toward Jody Racer and Super Rabbit Boy. Suddenly —

It's Princess Pirate and Robo Bobo! They go flying right over King Viking!

King Viking is very angry.

King Viking quickly catches up with Super Rabbit Boy and Jody Racer. Then he starts firing his fireballs.

Take this!

There are so many fireballs this time!
Super Rabbit Boy and Jody Racer have to
dodge them again . . .

and again . . .

and again . . .

But the fireballs keep coming! Soon Jody Racer and Super Rabbit Boy are crashing into each other to avoid being burned.

Super Rabbit Boy and Jody Racer forget about the fireballs. They are mad at each other! They start bashing and crashing into each other on purpose!

King Viking is pleased.

King Viking tries to speed past Super Rabbit Boy and Jody Racer. Just as he zooms between them, they swerve toward each other again!

9 PILEUP

It's a three-car pileup! King Viking, Jody Racer, and Super Rabbit Boy are in a pile in the middle of the road.

Suddenly King Viking is swooped off the ground. It's Robo Bobo and Princess Pirate! Team Viking is back on the track!

Oh no! King Viking is going to win!

It's the other racers! They've caught up in the race. Simon the Hedgehog, Frog Knight, and Nugget race ahead to catch up with King Viking.

Princess Pirate swings a super punch at Frog Knight. But Frog Knight uses his car's secret shield to bounce it right back at her!

Then Simon the Hedgehog uses his super spikes to pop Robo Bobo's tire.

King Viking flies into the air . . .

. . . and straight toward the finish line!

Suddenly Nugget is flying in the air, too! Her car has secret flying powers! She heads right for King Viking.

Nugget bashes into King Viking. The force blasts him out of the stadium and far, far away! Go, Nugget!

10 SURPRISE!

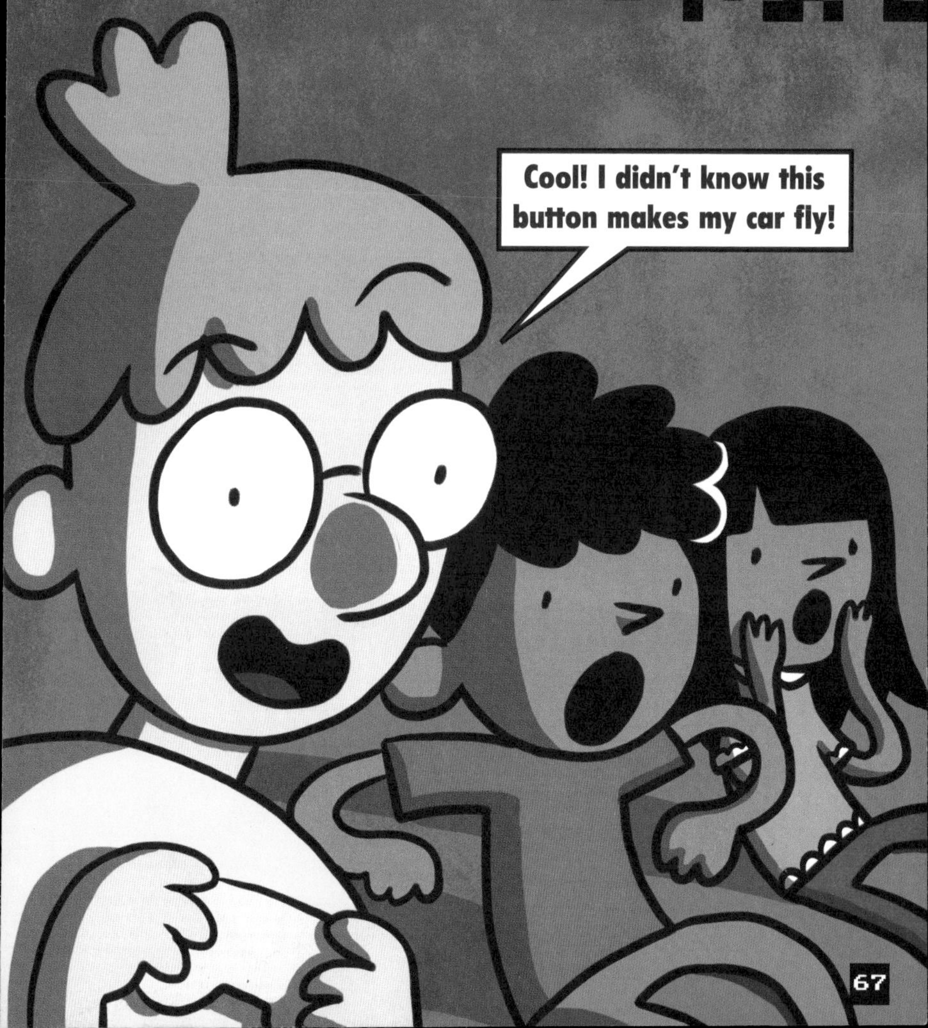

Nugget lands across the finish line — in first place!

Simon the Hedgehog takes second place. And Frog Knight takes third. Princess Pirate falls over the finish line in fourth.

That was the best race ever! What are the
final scores? Who won the Grand Prix?

```
                -THE SCORES-

1 NUGGET..................[+9]    18 POINTS
2 KING VIKING............[+0]    16 POINTS
3 JODY RACER.............[+0]    15 POINTS
4 SUPER RABBIT BOY......[+0]    15 POINTS
5 SIMON THE HEDGEHOG...[+6]     8 POINTS
6 FROG KNIGHT............[+3]     3 POINTS
7 PRINCESS PIRATE.......[+1]     1 POINTS
8 ROBO BOBO..............[+0]     0 POINTS
```

It's Nugget! She has won the Super Cup!

Cluck! Cluck!!

Everyone cheers for Nugget. Meanwhile, Super Rabbit Boy and Jody Racer apologize to each other.

THOMAS FLINTHAM

has always loved to draw and tell stories, and now that is his job! He grew up in Lincoln, England, and studied illustration in Camberwell, London. He now lives by the sea with his wife, Bethany, in Cornwall.

Thomas is the creator of THOMAS FLINTHAM'S BOOK OF MAZES AND PUZZLES and many other books for kids. PRESS START! is his first early chapter book series.

How to draw Super Rabbit Boy!

1.

2.

3.

4.

5.

SUPER FUNSTON

START
SELECT

Don't forget to sign your drawing!

THOMAS

PRESS START!

How much do you know about

SUPER RABBIT RACERS?

Look at pages 4 and 5. Use pictures to describe which character you would want to play.

Why does Jody Racer get mad at Super Rabbit Boy?

What are the four race courses in the Super Cup Grand Prix?

All of the cars in the race have a super secret power. Which power would you choose for your car?

Were you surprised by who won the Super Cup? Why or why not?

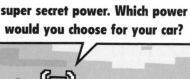

scholastic.com/branches